THE
ALCHEMIST
DAUGHTER

Paul S. Moore

THE
ALCHEMIST
DAUGHTER

THE ALCHEMIST DAUGHTER

T HE LOVE OF MY LIVES? I can't say. Love is a fuzzy thing. Blurs lines, it does ... There is one, different.

I met her while living a life of frolic and folly, filled with women and fleeting pleasures. I was a troubadour and never wanted to be any other thing.

Kings have told me, if not for love of country, they would want no other life but mine. Proof, again, that love is a fuzzy concept.

At the time of this story, I had never experienced a selfless love and, therefore, my opinions on the matter were shallowly held. Depth would come upon my arrival in the village of Densholme.

Densholme overlooked the King's farmland and bordered the Royal hunting forest. The village was prosperous. There were advantages to being just one day's carriage ride from the palace of King Henry, eighth in his line.

Henry fancied himself to be a troubadour and played well enough to be one. Having a taste for the young ladies, and a preference to believe he could woo them without the power of his authority, Henry often played and sang songs of seduction and romance. His musical reputation was a source of pride for him.

I took pride in being chosen to perform at a wedding attended by the King.

Upon arrival in Densholme, I made straight away to the home of Bram, the alchemist. It was he who had contracted with me to entertain at his daughter's wedding.

Bram sat sullen and pensive, surrounded by well-worn books, arranging vials of unlabeled ingredients atop his work table. He barely returned my greeting.

Bram explained his lack of cheer by telling of two daughters and two weddings.

Ella was smitten but unwise. Her groom was the rakish town crier. Like myself, he was a fool of a philanderer, possessing manly good looks and the brain of a pea hen.

Bram forbade the wedding, but he was made to relent, as the crier's sister was a favorite courtesan of King Henry. The king let it be known the marriage would be blessed by his attendance.

Just one year earlier, and to his regret, the alchemist had successfully prevented his eldest daughter, Hanna, from marrying a man of higher character, but lesser prospects.

This suitor had four years remaining on his indentured servitude agreement. He tended and harvested the wheat.

Ever vigilant to my own self-promotion, I saw opportunity. I made the father a promise, boasting, "I will write a special tune, an appropriate tune, to satisfy your wisdom to be heard, yet bless the wishes of the young lovers." I made the promise knowing full well I had already written and performed just such a song for many weddings.

After receiving my compensation, I headed for the inn. A dusty road requires a bath, hot food, a beverage, and a glance at the town's available damsels.

This inn was better than most. Being less than a day's ride from the palace gave it access to a more diverse and plentiful supply of foods and wines.

The dining area itself looked no different than others in the English woodlands. A dark room, dominated by a giant hearth, with a bubbling black pot, aromatically steaming, filled with soup made from whatever was in season.

I had no issue with my room, my bath, or the food. My fondest anticipation was for the after-meal visit to the tavern area of the Inn.

I caught sight of the serving wenches as they hurried past the door with pitchers of brew. One in particular caught my eye. Anticipation of conquest grew all the more at the sight of her.

Only one table in her area had an empty seat, next to a window with a view of a rolling valley of wheat fields.

Opposite the empty chair sat a weathered man in a dirty hemp shirt. He had the look of one who spent many years tending the fields. With his permission, I sat myself down and prepared my snare.

From beneath my jacket, I removed a parchment and quill. From my satchel, I removed my ink. No woman ever resisted asking me for what purpose those tools were used.

With my head down, ink pot out, parchment before me, and quill in hand, I sat. My eyes followed every move of the lovely lady. With trap set and baited, I waited.

"Looking like you are posing in a studious manner, to me," said the weathered man across the table. "Looking like you have designs on Hanna as well." He chuckled a little too long for my comfort.

"Begging pardon?" I bluffed.

"The girl with the flowing dress," he said, "The lady with sleeves the color of the almost ready wheat."

It was true. Her dress seemed more supple and colorful than the others. Its fabric, while not gossamer, might conceivably have been crafted by fairies. When she walked, her garment chased after her as if in a hurry to protect her figure from becoming exposed in its naked form.

I looked out the window at the freshly harvested sheaves of wheat. Once again, the weathered man was correct. The wheat was losing the dark green color of grass. The sleeves, hem, and neckline of her garment was a match for the lighter and quickly-fading green hue.

"You are an observant man," I said. "She and her dress are quite lovely. So, too, is your village at this time of year. I may stay until the leaves change their color."

Just at that moment, the maiden of our discussion appeared. She glanced at my parchment while asking the nature of my pleasure.

"Give my friend another round, and I will have one of the same, please."

"I thank you, pilgrim," he said, "but it is two hours before dark, and I have an early morning to attend." He winked at me and drained the remainder of his goblet.

As he stood to leave, he leaned into my ear and whispered, "You've met your match, sir."

I had only until the second draught arrived before she asked the nature of my writing. I told her I was going to perform at the wedding of the alchemist's daughter. I lied to her, telling her, "I have just composed a song specifically for the occasion."

"May I see it?" She asked me in a way that surprised me. I knew her motivation wasn't coyness. It didn't sound like curiosity. It was closer to … a need. I passed the parchment across the table, and she sat down in the empty chair.

The poem wasn't lengthy, but she took her time. Did she read it more than once? I asked her opinion and she lifted her head. A sweet smile lit her face, but tears trailed from both eyes.

"I like it very much, sir. My sister will like it as well."

"Your sister?" I was off my game now, feeling equally curious and adventurous.

"My sister," she repeated. "I too, am a daughter of the alchemist. In my mind, I feel like this was written for the both of us. I pray this will change my father's heart toward the man my sister loves. For me, it is too late."

"Too late?" I asked. "How so?"

"You are not the first troubadour to lure a woman with beautiful words, sir. I know what you want. I won't give it, but I can give you something better." She pointed past the window to a lone oak on a small rise overlooking the fields. "I will be done with my duties in one hour. If you come to the oak, I will show you how common things can be turned into silver and gold."

I couldn't refuse, and she met me beneath the oak at the time promised. I had brought my lute and she a bottle of wine.

Nature provided one of those fall evenings where the air itself energized the mind, and the sunset brought shifting colors to the hills. With the warmth of summer still held in the ground, the cool air held no threat of an uncomfortable chill in the body.

Again, I couldn't help but notice the movement of her dress as she crossed in front of me and settled under the tree. "Your garment," I told her, "Is the fairest dress ever worn by a maiden."

"You're kind to say so," she said. "I made it myself, softening the weave with ingredients in my father's cabinet."

"And did you dye the cloth as well?" I asked.

"Yes. I had in mind the colors of the village at this time of year. It was meant to be my wedding dress." A shiny wetness started to well in her eyes again, but she continued. "I was meant to be married at this time last year."

The way she spoke in low tones of sadness reminded me of the chords played by gypsies in their haunting songs of desire and loss.

This melancholy mood was not what I had hoped for. All I could do was change the conversation. "Would you care to hear a cheerful song?" I inquired.

"I would," she pleaded.

Hanna poured us both some wine, while I sang a silly ditty about a frog who crowed and a rooster who hopped, both in a journey to find the witch who enchanted them.

The silly tune seemed to help. Soon, we were trading stories. Me, of my adventures in far away places. She, of her love of the ingredients from far away places and the magical properties they held.

As time passed, I found myself speaking from my heart about feelings I had never before spoken. She spoke of wishes never fulfilled. I plucked at the lute while she spoke, and I felt she was singing her words. Thus was the level of pleasantness I felt when hearing her voice.

My reverie was interrupted by her sudden silence, then she touched my hand. "Look," she said, and pointed at the moon. "Now follow," she whispered and, still pointing, directed my eyes from the fullness of the moon, slowly down, until she stopped the motion of her hand, and I was looking at the sheaves in the field ... the sheaves that once had matched the coloring of her dress were now a shining silver under a dark sky and the light of the moon.

"I have made silver from the wheat of the field," she announced. Then she laughed like a child at play, and my heart, feeling moonstruck, ached to keep her for my own.

When again I spoke, sounds came out as a moan until I cleared my throat. "Tell me about the man you love," I said. "What is in him that can win the heart of a woman such as you?"

She had so many heartfelt reasons, and she shared them.

"His name is Evan. He is nothing like you," she announced, without any measure of cruelty. "The two of you could be best of friends. He has the ability to appreciate the talents in others that he, himself, does not possess, without jealousy or covetousness. A strapping, handsome man, inattentive to the ladies who look to him. He is a man who would find his greatest calling in building a world around his family. A friend, who would relish the advice, gently given, of a creative and industrious woman in the design of that life. He would protect that world with his own life, knowing what is right, and what is wrong. He has the courage to stand his ground. What he has no courage for is to take the woman he loves against the wishes of her father. For that I am heartbroken, and he is without his simple dream."

So, there it was. The mundane glory of a life worth living. The opposite of my own. The life I had run away from made madly appealing when the addition of this daughter of the alchemist could be imagined in it.

Hanna had taken one measure of my vanity, added another of my wanton lust, a pinch of my own selfish desires, and infused them with her own spirit, mixing a concoction inside of me that would burn in my heart for a lifetime.

I made myself the vow that I would forever forgo my desire to own her in conquest.

I wondered, against my own desires, if I could be of assistance in helping her attain the man she ached to marry.

Again, I changed the subject to things light and without consequence. We ended up laughing about the follies of the world, while I played a tune on the lute that seemed to sweeten the conversation with a melody enchanted by being near her. Its form came from songs I had heard while traveling in Spain. It's melody, not thought out or written, came from somewhere else. A place in my heart I never knew existed. Time was lost once more, until she suddenly held out a finger, pointing again at the wheat field.

"Look," she said. "As I promised."

The sun was coming up, its rays moving across the valley. As they moved, they enveloped the standing sheaves, and turned them, one by one, the yellow color of gold. She had kept her promise. In one night she had turned the common into silver and gold without benefit of enchantment or potions. She had turned my spirit, by enchantment alone, into a creature who plumbed the depth of a deeper love.

Now, I knew, I must keep my silent promise to help her find her happiness. Tomorrow evening was the wedding. At break of dawn, I waited at the door of her father's shop, eager to sing my song of the dutiful parent and love-struck daughter.

> *The sweetest of melons just slipped from the vine.*
> *From planting, through nurturing,*
> *Growing in time.*
> *Though I over-watered, she turned out just fine.*
> *She is the most beautiful thing*
> *I ever called mine.*
> *I would not have chose you to take her away,*
> *Yet there she stands, waiting, on her wedding day.*
> *After the dance where I give her away,*
> *Please take her, and hold her forever,*
> *Like you do today.*

He told me it was his thoughts, put to music.

"A double wedding, perhaps?" I asked. "I will not ask for more, in way of fee."

Life, having been a breeze from one selfish act to the next, didn't prepare me for what the father told me next. "If only my eldest daughter had not been claimed by our diseased king ..."

He didn't finish the statement. I had to pry the news from him.

"My daughter Hanna, upon hearing the King would attend her sister's wedding, took her own wedding dress from the chest to wash it. When the dress had dried, she wore it to the inn where she was given employ.

Among the eyes she caught that day was the king himself. Yesterday, I was informed he would take her for his bed. It is the king's will. Nothing can be done ... save this."

Bram opened his trembling hand and held out a vial containing a thin red liquid. I guessed his intent.

"It's for the King's wedding toast," he said.

"Stay that thought, good man." I implored him. "Don't bring evil to an unbalanced event. You may tip the balance to the devil's side."

"If I don't," he told me, "Evan would hang for a similar attempt, and all hearts would be lost to the devil's way of thinking. I know the man's mind."

"I, sir, know the mind of a troubadour," I countered. "The king fancies himself to be a troubadour at heart, and his deeds betray that he, indeed, is of that cloth. I can strike a bargain with him that will be smiled on by angels if you would relent."

I had so much to do, and I wasted little time.

After leaving Bram's shop, I went to see Hanna. She promised she would not wear the seductive dress to her sister's wedding. I told her it would best be left unworn until her own wedding ceremony with Evan.

She smiled without melancholy for the first time since I saw her. Hanna had made me a ridiculous promise carried out by moonlight and sunlight. I now had made her a promise to be carried out by the magical properties to be mined from the well of musical enchantment. I had a song to write, a performance to give, and a deal to be brokered.

I channeled the Spanish form, the magic of the previous evening, and the alchemical melding of variable light and basic nature. I wrote for the king a song of green sheaves and magic. I promised him he could call it his own if he would allow Hanna the freedom to choose her lover.

The rest is history.

Like all history, skewed, but still with some truth in the chaff. King Henry sold his rights to Hanna for a song. I called the song "Green Sheaves".

The words he changed greatly. His lyrics tell of a lovely prostitute who scorned his advances. The melody he changed not at all. The title he changed to "Green Sleeves". His changes betray that he long remembered his first vision of a maiden in a magical dress.

For myself? I was happy, yet melancholy, when asked during performances, "Do you know 'Green Sleeves'?" For me, it doesn't matter if I think of both song and woman. I play for my patron's pleasure, satisfied in knowing the song I bartered away to a king holds less value than what I let go for love.

ABOUT THE AUTHOR

Paul S. Moore was born in the Missouri Ozarks, raised in St. Louis, and eventually settled in the sand of central Florida. He calls each of these places home.

His inner mix of hillbilly river rat, lowlands daydreamer, sand road hermit, and reader of nineteenth-century history writers form the base of a non-elite education. These roots allow imagination to turn historic events into serendipitous thoughts. Those thoughts organize into stories, and stories become novels.

With the remedial help of a good critique group, and the birth of publishing companies that read a manuscript without asking first, "What are your credentials?", he's found a voice to share those stories.

ALSO BY THE AUTHOR

RULES OF THE CAMPFIRE

BOOK ONE FROM STORIES IN GLASS
by Paul S. Moore

If you woke up one day and realized you had memories from more than seventy lives, fluid in every language you'd ever spoken, and recalled all the texts you'd ever read, would you wonder why?

SONGS IN A BOX

BOOK TWO FROM STORIES IN GLASS
by Paul S. Moore

This time, the enemy is human.

BALLS IN PLAY

BOOK THREE FROM STORIES IN GLASS
by Paul S. Moore

Is it true that heroes are made, not born?

Available from Water Dragon Publishing in
hardcover, trade paperback, and digital editions
waterdragonpublishing.com/stories-in-glass

YOU MIGHT ALSO ENJOY

GREY MOTHER MOUNTAIN

by Elyse Russell

When her village is destroyed, an elderly woman seeks help from the last remaining dragon to get revenge.

PARRISH BLUE

by Vanessa MacLaren-Wray

Sallie never expected to discover a world she'd forgotten how to imagine.

THE THIRD TIME'S THE CHARM

by Steven D. Brewer

When an airship is hijacked by pirates, a young man with a secret loses his mentor ... and his future.

Available in digital and trade paperback editions from
Water Dragon Publishing
waterdragonpublishing.com/dragongems